Captain McGee and the
East Point Lighthouse

Doris E. Jargowsky

To order additional copies of this book, contact:
Xlibris
844-714-8691
www.Xlibris.com
Orders@Xlibris.com

ISBN: Softcover   978-1-4500-7275-5
            EBook   979-8-3694-0319-8

Print information available on the last page

Rev. date: 07/13/2023

Acknowledgement

"Captain McGee and the East Point Lighthouse"

won first prize in the first annual Delaware Bay

Day Poetry Contest. With Sally Starr standing next

to me, I began reciting the poem to an audience

consisting mainly of senior citizens, my mother,

Mildred Elbertson, among them.

Gather 'round children and listen to me,

While I tell you the tale of Captain McGee.

The captain, he was a quiet man,

And his love for the sea kept him off of the land.

Why, even his house on twelve pilings sat,

At the mouth of the river, like a welcome mat.

In the cool of the evening he would sit and rock,

By his trusty vessel, moored by the dock.

As each wave rolled back from lapping the shore,

He'd doze, then wake, and rock some more,

As another wave rose to slap the shore.

Oh, what a lullaby to endure.

And a wisp of a pup that he got from a friend,

Lay by his side, till the evening's end.

Early one morning, with that pup by his side,

He set sail for the sea on the ebbing tide,

Unaware of his fate on that day,

Or the turn of the tide, in his life on the bay.

For his thoughts were fixed far beyond the sea,

On his recent bride, named, Bonnie Lee.

A beautiful girl with eyes of blue,

But of her illness, he never knew.

Just a wisp of a girl with a pup by her side,

And it wasn't a week, when sweet Bonnie Lee died.

Captain looked at the pup, and then he sighed.

Then he revved up the engine to challenge the tide.

He sailed past East Point Light still shinning bright,

And turned away from Egg Island on his right.

Now the mackerel sky at the crack of dawn

Was the mirror image of the sea he was on.

And just when he felt so all alone,

He remembered the pup, and threw him a bone.

Captain looked at the thunderheads starting to form,

And he said to the pup, "They're brewing a storm."

Another knot to the engine's speed,

Its hesitation he did not heed.

And when the sea began to churn,

The Captain sailed on, refusing to turn,

While the pup paced the vessel, bow to stern,

Wondering what lesson he needed to learn.

Then, just when the wind had reached her peak,

Those clouds opened up and began to leak.

The pup continued his anxious pace

Until the sea slapped him in the face.

The pup was scared, he shivered and shook,

Curled up in a ball, and at the Captain did look.

15

The Captain then gave an angry shout,

And tried to turn the vessel about.

He grabbed the wheel with all his might,

For the wind, rain and current, he now had to fight.

But the tide was against him, and so was his fate.

He had traveled too far in his anger and hate.

Recanting his wish to join his mate,

He hoped against hope that it wasn't too late.

But the wind just laughed and waved her hand,

Blowing them further away from land.

In desperation, Captain dropped to his knees,

Looked toward Heaven, and cried, "Dear God please!"

"You know that I miss my sweet Bonnie Lee,

But look at this pup, he has no one but me!"

Well, what happened next was a total surprise,

For the Captain and pup both grew in size!

The Captain now stood over ten feet tall,

And he staid the helm to

fight the squall.

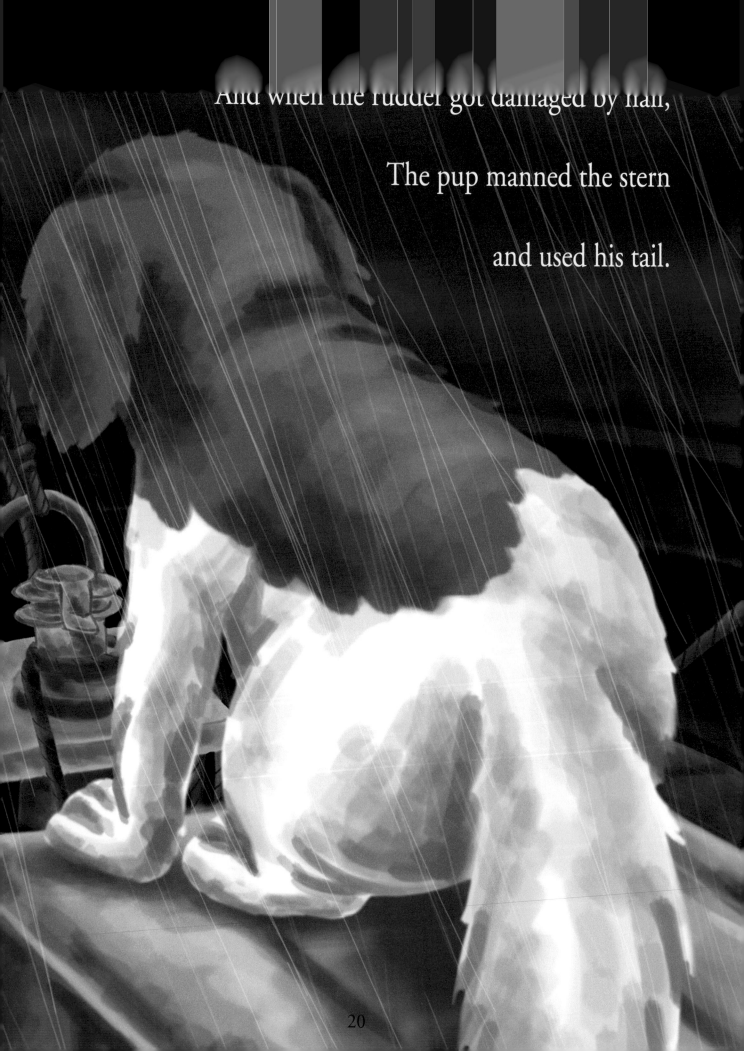

And when the rudder got damaged by hail,

The pup manned the stern

and used his tail.

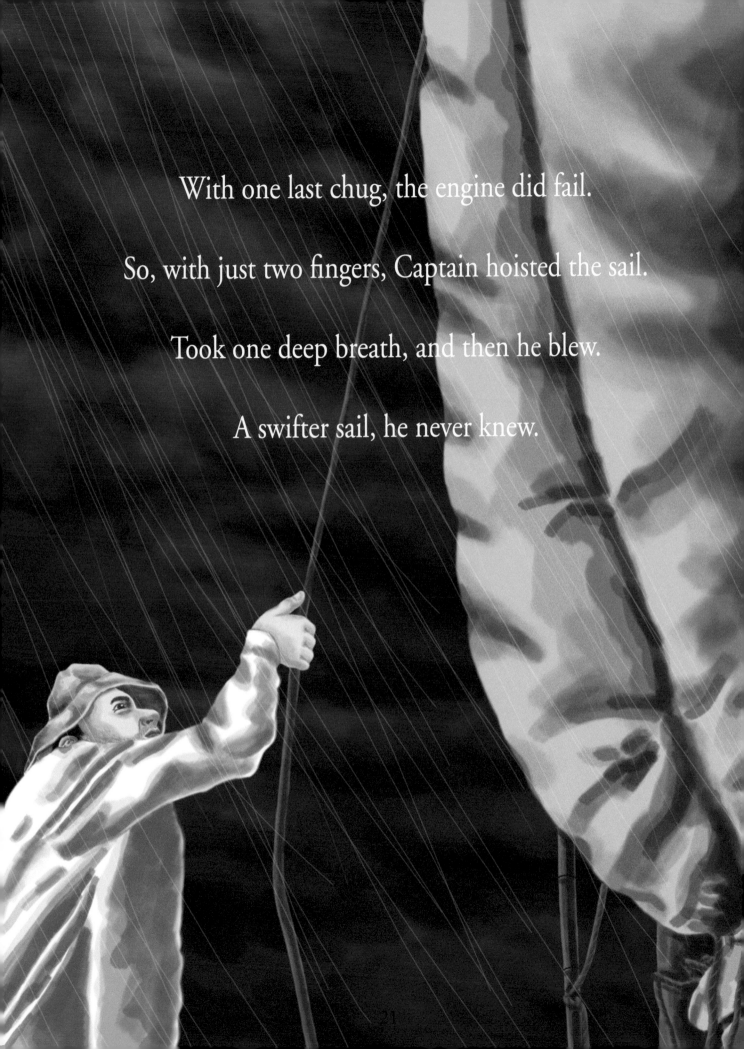

With one last chug, the engine did fail.

So, with just two fingers, Captain hoisted the sail.

Took one deep breath, and then he blew.

A swifter sail, he never knew.

When East Point Lighthouse came in sight,

Captain took out his bootlace and looped it tight.

Then, just like a cowboy in a rodeo,

He twirled it over his head and gave it a throw.

'Round East Point Light it took a hold.

Then the pup, now brave and bold,

Fearing not the sea beneath,

Grabbed that line between his teeth.

With just one yank, they reached the coast,

And used the lighthouse as a mooring post.

The townsfolk cheered and shouted a toast.

"Hooray, for the Captain, his pup is the most!"

Now, if it sounds like I'm bragging, it may well be.

For you see, my children, I'm Captain McGee.